Please visit www.kekespublishing.com for more information

ISBN: 978-1-7362892-0-4

Mama Means Business
Copyright © 2020
Kelly Bullock
All Rights Reserved.

Edited by Audrey Van Ryn
Proofread and edited by Sophie Call
Book design by Evgenija Burchak
Social Media by Ashley Causey-Golden
Website by Natalia Postrigan

Printed in USA
First edition, December 2020

To learn more about KeKe's Publishing, please visit my website at
https://www.kekespublishing.com

Merchandise and book activities are available online.

Please email KeKe's at kekespublishingllc@gmail.com with questions or comments.

KeKe's Publishing, LLC
Cincinnati, Ohio

Mama Means
Business

Dedication

I would like to dedicate this book to all my students. I have always encouraged you to exceed your potential. I used my own advice and self published my first children's book. Thank you for...

S haring your thoughts with me.

T eaching me how to teach you.

U nderstanding and meeting my high classroom expectations.

D oing your best always.

E njoying my class.

N ever giving up despite your challenges.

T hinking outside the box.

S howing up to learn everyday.

KeKe's Publishing, LLC
"Unlocking Potential and Opportunity Through Creativity"

Tonight was the biggest game of the year. Omari was worried about participating, because he needed to show Mama his report card.

Omari's mother, who sometimes felt like a single mom raising her three children, had always emphasized the importance of getting good grades. Both Mama and Dad reminded the children often that a good education would lead to future opportunities. Omari knew that if he didn't perform in the classroom, he wouldn't be allowed to perform on the field.

Education was always a top priority. That was the family motto, PERIOD! So he did what his friends encouraged him to do....

.... HIDE THE REPORT CARD!

It was Friday morning. "Time for school!" yelled Mama. "Come on, wake up!" she continued to yell while preparing breakfast and getting herself ready for work.

Omari wiped his eyes, slowly got up, and headed to the bathroom.

Nia and Lil D were hesitant about getting up.

"You both better get up!" Omari yelled. "I don't want to be late for school!"

"Hush, boy. You can't tell us what to do!" snapped Nia.

"You sure can't," Lil D groaned.

Mama raised her voice sternly one more time. "Let's go!"

The late starters quickly got up, got dressed, and headed to the kitchen for breakfast. The delicious aroma of Mama's cooking wafted through the air and filled the apartment: fluffy scrambled eggs, pancakes with chocolate chips and golden butter, cheese grits, turkey bacon, and Mama's homemade sweet rolls.

"Yummy, Mama!" shouted Lil D. "Are we having a special breakfast or something?"

"Yes," Mama replied. "Omari has a big game tonight. I want to make sure he starts his day off with a good meal."

Just then, Omari began to look pale and worried.

"Are you okay?" asked Mama. "Do you feel sick?"

"No," Omari explained, "I'm just tired."

Nia knew that wasn't the truth and gave him a dirty look, rolling her eyes and poking him under the table with her feet.

After breakfast, the kids finished getting

6

ready for school and Mama prepared for work.

"Have a great day," said Mama, as she kissed each of them on the forehead. "Watch out for cars and look both ways before you cross the street."

"Okay, we will, Mama," replied Nia, as she waved, watching Mama pull away.

Ameera and Diego met them outside as usual, and they began walking to school.

"Did you tell your mom?" asked Diego.

"No!" replied Omari.

"What are you waiting on?" Ameera said sarcastically.

"I'm not going to tell her right now, maybe later," said Omari. "If I tell her now, then I won't be able to play in the SuperBowl tonight!"

"She's going to find out. Mama always does," said Lil D.

"You're going to be in big trouble," sighed Diego.

Mama arrived at work and began preparing for an important meeting. She stuck her hand down beside her desk abruptly, feeling for her canvas tote bag. But it wasn't there!

Now beginning to panic, Mama said angrily, "I can't believe it! I left it at home! What am I going to do?"

She sat in her office chair and stared at the wall for a minute, in deep thought. She didn't want to, but knew right away that she had to go back home.

Mama walked to her boss's office. "Mr. Wallace, I'm so sorry. I'll be back in thirty minutes. I left my work bag at home."

Mama could tell from the look on his face that Mr. Wallace was not happy.

Mama got in the minivan and drove back to the apartment. She ran up the steps quickly, unlocked the door, and retrieved her bag. Moving hastily, she dropped the keys while locking the door. As she leaned down to pick them up, she noticed a blue and white backpack in the corner.

Mama pursed her lips and took a long, deep breath. It was Omari's! She paused for a minute while trying to decide if she should drop it off at the school on her way back to work or just forget about it. She set her belongings down, picked it up, and decided to rummage through it.

The backpack was disgusting! There were crumbs, candy wrappers, an empty juice box, and several papers that Omari clearly hadn't given to her. She noticed in one of the pockets a small, thick piece of paper that had been folded several times. She opened it and realized it was Omari's report card!

Mama scanned the report card and quickly became agitated. She was not happy with what she saw. The more she read, the angrier she became. It was as if steam was coming from her ears!

Omari's mom sat for a moment in disbelief, thinking about her next move. Instead of dropping it off at school, she decided to leave a note at home for the children.

Mama headed back to work. She could hardly focus during the meeting because she was so upset. She was thinking about the conversation she was going to

Dear Kids,

I am very disappointed in you! Not telling the truth comes with consequences. Please power off all your cell phones and tablets, unplug your game system and place the controllers along with all electronic devices on my dresser. See you at 4:30

With love,

Mama

have with them when she got home.

After school, the kids met at the stop sign to walk home together.

Nia noticed Omari didn't have his backpack with him. "Where is your backpack?" she asked.

"I don't know. I think I left it at home."

"You what!" Nia said with great surprise. "Did you turn in your homework?"

"No, I had a horrible day, and Coach JT said that I have to turn it all in before the game tonight or I can't play."

"You're not going to play anyway when Mama finds out!" declared Lil D.

Omari gave his big brother a scary look, and then threw the straw he had been chewing at him.

The kids arrived home. Diego and Ameera headed towards their apartments.

"Bye!" they all said.

Lil D noticed that Ameera's parents were barbequing on the balcony. "Ask your dad if I can get a dog with barbeque sauce and mustard."

"No, you ask him. You have a mouth," Ameera said, as she closed the door firmly.

The three siblings continued walking to their own apartment.

What a surprise they were about to encounter!

As soon as their apartment door closed, they all knew right away something was wrong.

Omari stood frozen to the spot. He

could see his backpack sitting in Mama's favorite chair, papers spread all over the coffee table and a note on the refrigerator, written in big letters on a piece of cardboard.

"Come quick!" said Lil D.

They all stared at the note.

"Why are we all in trouble?" moaned Lil D. He got in Omari's face. "You're the one who didn't tell the truth!"

"Yeah, if you had taken your backpack to school, then this would have never happened." Nia rolled her eyes and walked away with Lil D.

Omari remained standing in front of the refrigerator in disbelief, staring at the note. He was very worried about what he had done.

Mama always had a routine for her children to follow when they came home from school. First, they had to put any papers from school in the kitchen tray.

Next, they could choose a snack and have 30 minutes of "me time." Finally, they had to start their homework and make sure it was completed by the time she came home.

Today was going to be a different kind of a day. They knew they had to start their routines, but they also had to follow Mama's demands.

They quickly followed the request in the note, sadly putting all their electronics on Mama's dresser. Then, they began working on their homework. Omari was so nervous that he could hardly concentrate.

The apartment door opened. You could hear a pin drop. The kids were at the kitchen table working. They all paused in what they were doing.

Lil D got up quickly and approached Mama. "We can explain!"

"Save it for someone who wants to hear it!" Mama said as she walked toward her room to put down her work bag.

Lil D was stunned!

"Why did you say something to her?" growled Nia.

"Because I wanted to. We can't just ignore what happened."

Omari remained at the table with his head down, wondering what Mama was going to do or say.

They could all hear muttering coming from the bedroom. Mama was on the phone with someone. But who?

Mama entered the kitchen and placed the phone in the center of the table, tapping the speaker button so everyone could hear. "Hello," said a deep,

familiar voice.

The children's eyes suddenly got big! "Dad!" they all said in unison, with both excitement and trepidation. Their dad was in the military and had been gone for almost a year. They all missed him very much.

"Yes, it's me! It's great to hear your voices, but I am disappointed that we have to talk under these circumstances. What were you all thinking?!" he said, with his voice raised.

"Obviously, they weren't thinking," said Mama angrily.

"Whose bright idea was it to hide the report card?" asked Dad.

Nia and Lil D pointed towards Omari at exactly the same time.

"Haven't we taught you all about the importance of being honest, ALWAYS, no matter what?"

Omari jumped in quickly. "I'm sorry. It was all my fault. I begged them not to tell on me. Really, I did."

"So what? That doesn't make it right!" yelled Mama. "They are just as guilty as you are. Birds of a feather flock together!"

"Mama and I are really upset with the decisions you all have made!" came Dad's voice on the phone. "Therefore, you will all be given consequences for your actions. I have to get back to work now."

"Dad, can I play in the game tonight?" Omari asked anxiously.

Dad didn't even answer.

Omari stomped all the way to Mama's favorite chair and sat down hard with his head down.

Mama hung up the phone and marched right after him. With a stern look and a harsh tone, she said, "You'd better straighten up and fly right!"

Lil D and Nia sat at the table, feeling bad for not telling the truth. Mama had always used that phrase with her children, but they didn't quite understand the meaning. They only knew that when she said it, Mama meant business!

Just as Mama was getting ready to give out the punishments, her phone rang. Mama headed to her bedroom.

"Hello!"

"Hi, Mrs. Mitchell. It's JT, Omari's coach. I was calling to let you know that your son did not turn in his signed report card and according to his teacher, he is missing three assignments."

"I know. I'm very frustrated with him!" said Mama.

"We have a game tonight and we need him to play."

"Thanks for calling, coach. I found the papers hidden in his backpack. He has been punished, but I'm not done with him yet. Yes, Omari will be at the game tonight, but in a different capacity," Mama said sternly.

Coach JT was a bit confused, but didn't dare ask her what she meant. Mama's tone was serious and scary at the same time.

He paused and then said, "Okay, great. See you soon."

Omari was eavesdropping on Mama's conversation through the bedroom door. His eyes were wide and he was grinning from ear to ear. He had heard Mama say that he would be at the game.

He ran and told his siblings.

"No way," said Nia.

"Yes way," replied Omari.

"But Mama and Daddy were really mad!" said Lil D. "I can't believe it!"

"Well, believe it. Get ready, we're leaving soon," Omari said happily, as he walked away.

Then Mama yelled out, "We are leaving in fifteen minutes! Pack up your backpacks and bring them with you!"

"Why?" said Nia, with her face all scrunched up. "I wonder if Mama is feeling okay. Who takes their school backpack to a football game?"

Lil D shook his head, with a puzzled look on his face.

There was no response from Mama.

They all got in the minivan and drove to the game. Omari was already dressed in his football uniform. Mama pulled into the parking lot at the field and the kids quickly got out, excited to see their friends. Mama told them to meet her in twenty minutes by the concession stand. It was her turn to volunteer.

When they arrived at the designated location, they were confused by what they saw … THREE DESKS! Two were inside the concession area and the other one was next to the bleachers, very close to the players' bench.

"Omari, you will not be playing in the game tonight!" Mama explained, handing each of them their backpack, "Instead, your desk is waiting for you. You will complete all of your missed assignments while supporting your team during the game."

Omari immediately felt sick to his stomach.

"Nia and Lil D, you will be working on the extra credit assignments that I created for you."

"Why, Mama?" whined Lil D, with watery eyes.

"What did we do?" asked Nia, in a shaky voice.

"You all broke the family rule by covering up your brother's bad actions. We will discuss it when we get home, but for now, get to work."

Omari was upset. He fought hard to keep the tears from rolling down his cheeks as he made his way to the desk.

His teammates encouraged him with pats on his shoulder pads.

"It will be okay," said Diego. "We are going to win this game!"

The game started! Chattering, loud cheers, whistles blowing, and the smell of popcorn were in the air.

Suddenly, a roar of what sounded like fireworks came from the sky, but there was no rain, just gray gloomy clouds everywhere.

"Oh no," thought JT. "I hope it doesn't start to rain."

The prospect of rain was exciting to Omari. He was hoping that the game would be postponed and he would get a chance to play. He kept working at the desk, wishing he was taking part in the game.

Lil D and Nia finished their work at the same time.

"Mama, can we go play now?" asked Lil D.

"Yes, but we are going to talk later about what you both could have done differently."

They gave her a hug and ran off.

Omari noticed them playing. He approached Mama. "Mama, may we talk?"

"Yes," she said.

Omari and Mama took a walk. He apologized for what he had done.

Mama explained to him that not telling the truth really hurts the person who fibbed.

Omari assured Mama that he would never do it again.

His mom hugged him and accepted his apology.

"Mama?"

"Yes, Omari."

"Any chance I could play in the game?"

"Well, I'll see."

They walked toward the sideline of the game where Mama and Coach JT had a conversation. Omari had his fingers crossed.

It was the fourth quarter and the Little Keys were losing by three. Both Mama and Coach JT looked at Omari.

"Suit up!" said the coach. It was music to Omari's ears. He was ready to cry, happy tears, of course.

Omari ran out on the field. He and the quarterback exchanged pats on their helmets. It was second down and the team needed a big play.

"Hut!" The ball was snapped and Omari ran with it for five yards.

The fans had hope. The Little Keys needed six more yards to score. The time clock was running down.

"Hut!" Omari gave it his all! But, despite his best efforts, he came up short.

The game ended and Omari's team lost. Everyone was so disappointed, especially Omari. His family rallied around him with encouragement and hugs.

Mama said, "Omari, there's always next year. Keep your head up." She put her arms around him with a big, tight squeeze.

Omari felt so bad. He knew that his team had paid a price because of his actions.

Lightning streaks began to flash brightly in the sky. A sudden burst of rain caused the crowd to scatter rapidly from the field.

Mama and the children ran quickly to the minivan.

The kids thought that they were going home, but Nia noticed that something about the ride was unusual. Mama was taking a different route! In fact, she was headed in the opposite direction from home!

Lil D asked, "Why are we going this way? Are we not going home?"

Mama replied, "Sit back and relax. It's a surprise!"

Find out what happens next in Book 2!

Please visit my website at https://www.kekespublishing.com

Author's Note

Thank you God for blessing me with the "Fruits of the Spirit"... Love, Joy, Peace, Patience, Kindness, Goodness, and Self-Control.

Darrell – I love the story of us! Twenty four years of miles and memories. Our journey will only get stronger. Hugs and Kisses!!!

Daddy – I love and miss you with all my heart! RIP- I know you are smiling down on me saying, "Look at Dooper".

Mom – You are the strength of our family. Your sacrifices will always be cherished. I love you to the moon and back!

Lil Darrell, Nia, Omari- The three of you make my life complete. Love you always!

Madison and Deuce – You are the joy of my life. You make KeKe smile!

Cheryl, Jim Jim, Kim, and Calvin – I love the sibling bond we share. It could never be broken! Love you!

Thank you to the rest of my beautiful family and friends for your love and support. It means the world to me!